# HEY, PRESTO!

Nadia Shireen

Alfred A. Knopf
New York

For
Linus

THIS IS A BORZOI BOOK PUBLISHED BY ALFRED A. KNOPF

Copyright © 2012 by Nadia Shireen

All rights reserved. Published in the United States by Alfred A. Knopf, an imprint of Random House Children's Books, a division of Random House, Inc., New York. Originally published in hardcover in Great Britain by Jonathan Cape, an imprint of Random House Children's Books, a division of the Random House Group Limited, London.

Knopf, Borzoi Books, and the colophon are registered trademarks of Random House, Inc.

Visit us on the Web! randomhouse.com/kids

Educators and librarians, for a variety of teaching tools, visit us at randomhouse.com/teachers

Library of Congress Cataloging-in-Publication Data is available upon request.
ISBN 978-0-375-86905-1 (trade) — ISBN 978-0-375-96905-8 (lib. bdg.)

The illustrations in this book were created using pencil, ink, collage, and digital rendering.

MANUFACTURED IN CHINA
November 2012
10 9 8 7 6 5 4 3 2 1

First American Edition

Presto and Monty didn't have much, but it didn't matter.
They were best friends and they were happy.

twang
twang
twang

Monty was good at singing,

eating ice cream

and making extremely silly faces,

while Presto had a most unusual talent.
With the help of a battered old hat
and a slightly wonky wand . . .

. . . he was a brilliant MAGICIAN.

One day, Monty saw a poster that made him *very* excited. "We'll put on a magic show and become famous!" he hooted.

So they packed up Presto's battered old hat and slightly wonky wand, and set off.

When they got there,
the carnival was quite busy.

"I know!" said Monty, bouncing up
and down. "We should take turns
being the star of the show. I'll go first."

So Monty shouted in his loudest voice,

ROLL UP, ROLL UP!

hook-a-duck

Presto hid behind him and made sure all the magic tricks worked perfectly.

Presto waited patiently for his turn to be onstage. But it never seemed to happen. It was Monty's turn, night . . .

after night . . .

after night. . . .

The magic show was a great
success. But something odd
had happened to Monty.

He had become bossy,

rude and demanding.

Presto wasn't enjoying himself anymore.

Soon, thanks to Presto, Monty was famous.
He was offered a big bag of money to put on
THE BIGGEST MAGIC SHOW EVER.
It would even be on television.

"I'm going to be a *superstar*!"
said Monty. "And this time, Presto,
you'll even get to be onstage!"

But Presto didn't want to be sawn
in half–ESPECIALLY by Monty.
He picked up his battered old hat and
his slighty wonky wand, and left the
carnival for good.

The next day, it was

**SHOWTIME!**

"Hey, Presto!"
Monty called.
But his friend
had disappeared.

"Humph," said Monty. "Well, I'm the star around here. Who needs him anyway?"

He bought himself a shiny new hat,

found a very fancy magic wand

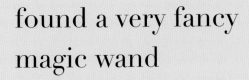

and quickly read a big book about magic tricks.

Back at home, Presto wondered if
Monty didn't need him after all.

But Monty's show didn't
get off to a good start. . . .

# And it went from bad . . .

. . . to worse.

Presto couldn't bear it
any longer.

Monty knew his time as a
famous magician was over.
But that wasn't why he felt sad.
"Oh, Presto!" said Monty.
"I wish you were here. What a
terrible friend I've been."

EASY PEASY MAGIC

But then . . .

HEY, PRESTO!

Presto finally made his entrance.

The crowd went wild.

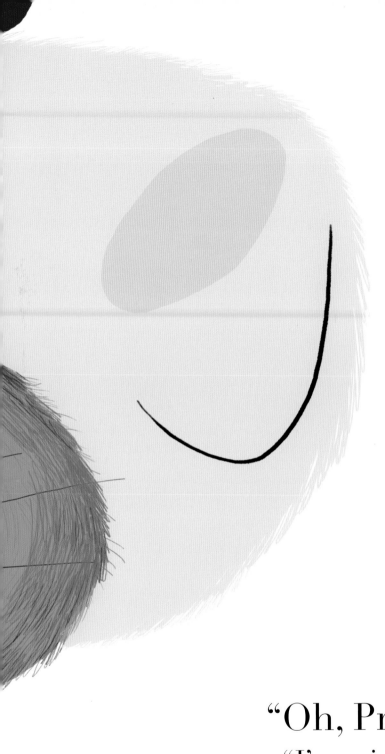

"Oh, Presto!" said Monty.
"I've missed you so much!"

Presto gave a contented purr, and
Monty promised that things would
be different from now on.

And that's how the friends
cooked up a brand-new act

OooooH!

PRESTO &

and found that, together . . .

. . . they put on the perfect show.